Henry D. Stevens

A Boy's Life

Its Spiritual Ministry

Henry D. Stevens

A Boy's Life
Its Spiritual Ministry

ISBN/EAN: 9783337334512

Printed in Europe, USA, Canada, Australia, Japan

Cover: Foto ©Andreas Hilbeck / pixelio.de

More available books at **www.hansebooks.com**

A BOY'S LIFE

Its Spiritual Ministry

BY

HENRY D. STEVENS

The spirit only can teach.
—*Emerson.*

BOSTON

JAMES H. WEST CO., PUBLISHERS

TO

ARTHUR'S BROTHER RALPH,

THIS LITTLE BOOK

OF PRECIOUS MEMORIES.

CONTENTS

ARTHUR helped in the writing of this story of a Boy's Life. Indeed, he is the author of it far more than I; for he first *lived so beautifully* that it made the telling of this true story of his life possible; and then his memory, when he was gone, became the spiritual influence that prompted to its writing. Lastly, the thought of him, of all he has been to me, and is, has urged me to make this acknowledgment of my precious indebtedness.

INTRODUCTORY WORD.

WHY should not the story of a boy's life be written as well as the life of a man? Has he not lived and acted, thought and suffered, and known serious experiences? It is certain that a boy lives his first years more keenly alive to the things about him than does the adult man. Children are very much alive; they are fresh and as yet unspoiled human nature. No coarse experiences have removed the bloom from their thoughts, no love for the sordid things of life has crowded out its finer meanings. The great wonder at the beautiful world into which they have been so unconsciously ushered still glistens in their eyes, and they live a charmed life in a real world, seeing much of the beauty and feeling much of the poetry of it, fresh as from the hand of God.

Are we not far too unconscious of the spiritual meaning and emotional education for us of the lives of the boys and girls living in the familiar intimacies of our own households? Too painfully true is it that we do not reverently recognize them as God-sent, and are often unaware of the value and extent of their delicate ministry. In truth, they bring to us our deepest joys, our tenderest happiness, and those emotional experiences which, lying deepest, are unforgettable. Indeed, they mould us fully as deeply as we mould them, and in ways very essential to our highest spiritual growth.

As I look back at Arthur's short life of only sixteen years, I find in its incidents and events nothing that sets it outside the ordinary lives of other boys. It was simple and healthful,— the gradual unfolding of a boy's nature and the development of his character amid the usual experiences of American family life. But there was a nobility of impulse and motive in it, and a sweetness of spirit about it, which was unmistakable. It was my blessed privilege to have known this transparent soul, and to have lived with him in the sacred intimacy of family life. It was not only the parental and filial, but also the spiritual friendship of father and son,— a oneness of spirit that was felt and enjoyed by both, and that drew us together in closest sympathy in all our common experiences. What that life has been to me forms a secret chapter illustrative of the spiritual influence of one life upon another. In him was to be seen and felt what is humanly meant by "the beauty of holiness." His character *taught*, by its presence; his spirit became a ministry in itself. And knowing how suggestive, helpful and constraining an influence it has been, how deeply rooted in the spiritual life were its lessons, I have thought that others might be aided and inspired by its brief recital. The gracious ministry of his short life, broken in earthly form though it be, may thus be widened and find entrance into other lives by the power of example and incitement.

Because of this dear boy I knew, all boys to me are fair; and I look at them in hopeful expectancy, to watch the coming forth of their diviner promise. If this simple narrative of a real boy's experiences and influence shall help others to lead more beautiful and helpful lives, both Arthur and I will be glad together.

H. D. S.

PART I.

PICTURES AND INCIDENTS.

Heaven lies about us in our infancy.
—*Wordsworth.*

Children are God's apostles, day by day
Sent forth to preach of love, and hope, and peace.
—*Lowell.*

Child-heart— mild-heart !
Ho, little wild heart !
Come up here to me out o' the dark,
Or let me come to you !
—*James Whitcomb Riley.*

Fair are the children and the flowers,
But their subtle suggestion is fairer.
—*Richard Realf.*

Great, wide, beautiful, wonderful world,
With the wonderful water round you curled,
And the wonderful grass upon your breast,—
World, you are beautifully drest.
—*W. B. Rands.*

Blessed childhood, which brings down something
of heaven into the midst of our rough earthliness.
—*Amiel.*

(12)

A BOY'S LIFE.

PART I.

PICTURES AND INCIDENTS.

I.

THE HUMAN TIE.

Of all the places on earth
I'd rather have had for my birth,
None is half so full of bliss
As dear old Indianapolis.

THESE simple lines were found pencilled in
Arthur's handwriting in a school note-book.
They seem to have been written to express his
strong preference for the actual place of his
birth over all other possible birth-places; and we
feel sure he thus sought to express in this artless

rhyme his special love for this inland city where
he was born and spent most happily the first six
years of his life.   Other places he liked and
enjoyed, but this seemed more like home to his
boyish recollections than any of the other places
of our residence.

Probably his pleasantest memory of this home-
city life was connected with the last house in
which we lived.   It was a small, low, brown
cottage in a large yard and surrounded by a
profusion of trees, shrubs and flowering plants.
Here were fruit-trees and grape-vines and berries
in abundance, and the quiet seclusion which is
possible about the last house on the street.   It
was like living in the country, and yet we felt
enough of the stir and life of the city about
us to overcome the sense of isolation.   Here
were large, open spaces of greensward for play-
ground, and all that wealth of material for
play-purposes which makes glad the heart of
children.   Under the maple-trees hung a swing,
while the notes of the meadow-lark came cheerily
up from the meadow below.   It was a home-like
and true nesting-place for the opening wonder
and vivid imaginations of young childhood,
and here the longest and happiest days known

in the lives of our children were spent. It was the one idyllic experience for us all; for the parents shared with their children the enjoyment of its natural freedom and secluded happiness. We were made to recall for ourselves the gladly-remembered ecstasy of our childhood-days, seeing it lived over again in our own children, and could easily enter by a re-awakened sympathy into that never to be repeated experience of theirs—

"When the heart beats young and our pulses leap
        and dance,
With every day a holiday and life a glad romance."

It was our earthly Paradise, and the only regret now is that we did not then more fully and keenly realize what it held for us all.

He had been very sick. It was the dreaded scarlet-fever that had sent its poisonous germ-emissaries to lay siege to the little citadel of his health. He was at that time the only victim of its malign activity; we knew not whence it came, no one could trace it to its deadly lair. For days and weeks it had slowly undermined his strength

and wasted his vitality. His body had shrunken
to a skeleton. I was sitting one morning holding his loved body in my arms, when suddenly
upon the March air the untamed notes of a bag-
pipe drifted indistinctly into the room. Nearer
and clearer they came. I was strangely affected,
even fascinated, in listening to these sounds, so
unfamiliar to American ears; and something in
them carried a vaguely prophetic meaning — an
elusive suggestion of impending calamity. It
distressed me, and I was glad when it was gone.
The days that followed were days of deepest
anxiety. The little life seemed to droop lower
and lower. His pulse was at the danger-point —
the doctor could offer no hope. We were preparing ourselves for the impending worst. Tenderest affection had done its best service. Sleepless
days and nights for weeks had been gladly
accepted for the dear boy's sake, but skill and
affection seemed equally helpless and hopeless.
And there, as he again lay, one never to be forgotten morning, on my arm, we alone in the
room, my spirit fell upon its face before what
seemed the inevitable loss and the just demand
of violated Nature. And then I thought it all
over,— of what his life had been to me, short as

it was, of what all its precious promise to me might mean in the years to come, of all my need of his life,— because *I loved him so.* And then, if ever I prayed, my prayer ascended to the Father-Life of us all, pleading with all the earnestness a father can feel, that my dear baby boy's life should be spared to me now, even if only for just a little while longer — a few years more, I urged. If it were best, yea, if only it were possible, I asked the granting of this gift to my life; that this deep prayerful longing of my inmost heart be not denied me. My hope trembled, but it was still hope. Then a peace seemed to come over me; I had done all I could.

The climax of his disease had been reached, a change came, and it was — oh, joyous consciousness — a change for the better. It seemed that my heart's beseeching was to be fulfilled. His little fluttering breast, that for long days had been like a frightened bird's, began to grow less agitated, the fever loosened the deadly persistency of its hold, and soon the dear boy could sleep upon a pillow, instead of upon my shoulder where he had lain and lived for weeks. Slowly came back the healthier pulse of a renewed life;

and with yearning hope we nursed the little life, which had been trembling on the danger-line, to a recovery of nearly its former strength.

Although thus spared to us at this time, the effects of this poisonous disease remained, and was probably the main cause of all his later sickness and ill-health.

One incident of these days of convalescence is treasured up as a pleasant memory. After he had recovered sufficiently, he was allowed to run out of doors; and upon one tonic April morning, the sun shining brightly, he sped gleefully out along a path through the yard, a tassel dangling from his Turkish cap as he ran back and forth, and feeling keenly the joy of once again being alive and able to play. As he drew near on one of his return trips, he warbled out, with an inimitable cadence of happiness, to us who stood watching him, these words: *"I love the pretty sunshine!"*

This seemed his veritable song of praise for restoration to health, and in it he seemed also to have compressed his love for the brightness

of these spring days and for the goodness of life.
This little incident illustrates his habitual attitude, throughout his whole life.   He looked for
and loved the beautiful things in life, and he
turned towards its sunshine as naturally as would
a flower, enjoying its warmth and brightness as
only a sensitive nature could.   The joy in his
heart was met and answered by those scenes in
Nature upon which the sunshine lavished her
prodigal wealth of life and hope.

II.

"I'M HOME AT LAST."

WHEN about four years of age Arthur went to spend one day, in Summer, with his grand-parents. The day was very warm, and the distance about half a mile. His father left him happy at their house, and, by agreement, was to call for him later in the day, when returning from his work.

Arthur had never been away from home before for such a length of time, and so this became a very memorable event in his boyish life. He spent several hours very happily with "grandma's folks," but, the day proving longer than he had expected, he at length grew thoughtful and restless and tired of his amusements, and said he would like to go home. They tried to persuade him to wait until "papa" came, but that seemed too long a time to wait, for this anxious and now thoroughly homesick little boy. And so, bidding them "good-by," he started home alone, along streets and through cross-lots, by the same route he had taken in the morning.

He must have walked rapidly, as his desire to get home had now grown more intense. He then truly experienced what is meant by "the heat and the burden of the day," for he was tired, heated, and worried about getting home, and this little trip must have seemed to him as long as one of many miles to an older person. He evidently became quite discouraged during the trip,— at its apparently increasing length, and at the slowness of his progress; for no doubt his desire to get home more than kept pace with his short, boyish steps. Is it possible for us of older years to fully appreciate the agitation, doubt and fear which filled the mind of this little boy of four, as he trudged along on that hot summer afternoon in hope of soon reaching the end of his homeward journey? Only the sympathy of imagination can tell us, for the trials of childhood are in truth as great, to the children concerned, as are life's later experiences to those who meet them in their maturer years.

But at last the seemingly long journey drew to an end, as the little brown cottage among the trees known as " home " came into sight and his dusty feet hurried through the gateway. Panting still with excitement, with his large eyes full of the most serious gaze,— with a sigh of satisfaction as at an escape from some awful fate, and with a never to be forgotten tone of pathos, he exclaimed to his mother, as he caught sight of her face, —*"I'm home at last!"*

III.

IT was to be a Sunday-school picnic up the river, on a beautiful steamboat. Our Sunday-school and a neighboring one had joined numbers and enthusiasm for the occasion, and a most delightful outing was in prospect.

To all of our family it was then a refreshing novelty, while, for our two boys, it was to be an experience transferred from out the dreamland of boyhood's imagination into the rare enjoyment of actual realization. What an exhilarating experience it was, as we stood on the temporary landing or wharf on the river-bank above Moline, and saw the "White Swan," gay with flags and bunting, and resounding with band-music, come ploughing and puffing through the swift current of the Mississippi river, directly towards us! It was a sight to stir the blood of enjoyment

in veins less rapid than those of childhood —
it made us all young together. As we walked
on board, the boat seemed like a huge bird of
festivity which was going to allow us to ride on
her back as she sped up the river, sailing proudly
and easily on the bosom of the Father of Waters.

The picnic rendezvous was only a few miles dis-
tant, and the trip just long enough to pass a few
islands and to catch glimpses of the little ham-
lets upon either shore. Soon the boat swung to,
upon the Iowa bank, and "tied up" opposite a
smooth plateau of ground covered with scattered
groves, and through one side of which ran a
small brook that emptied its tiny thread of life
into the great current. The older people and
youths and maids at once sought the shelter of
the trees, while the children scattered about in
all directions, seeking various forms of personal
enjoyment, a good deal as butterflies flit about
over flower-laden fields for the choicest sweets.
Some, already hungry, went to sample the lunch-
baskets; some began playing ball and croquet,
while others fitted up swings and hammocks.

Our boys had come especially prepared for
fishing. To catch a good-sized fish out of that
big river would be such a notable feat for small

boys who had always lived inland! and therefore this became the one engrossing ambition for the hour. Getting the tackle in order, they were soon seated upon the river-bank at the point where the brook suddenly lost its being in the yellow, muddy waters, and cast in their lines. Arthur had not been waiting long in this patient manner for results, when, as a result of watching the swiftly-rolling water, he suddenly became dizzy, lost his balance, and plunged headlong into the river, which at this point was quite deep. He could not swim; and, the accident happening so unexpectedly, it would have been quite natural for so young a boy to lose his presence of mind and run the great risk of being drowned.

Some one cried out that Arthur had fallen into the river. What did he himself do? For one thing, he did not lose his self-possession, but exercised his usual habit of being cool and self-poised. He told us afterwards that, as soon as he became conscious of what had happened, and realized that he was down under the water, he thought of the danger of strangling; and at once there came into his mind the advice which his Sunday-school teacher had given the class of which he was a member: namely, whenever thrown under the water, to shut the lips tightly together and hold the breath. This he did, and by so doing soon managed to come to the surface without getting water in his lungs, and was ready and able to grasp the extended hand of his older brother, who had now come to his rescue. This action of Arthur's,— considered and carried out under the water,— had doubtless saved his life; and it is illustrative of that habitual calmness, and thoughtfulness of demeanor under exciting circumstances, which were always conspicuous in his career.

The pleasure of that Sunday-school picnic, so bright in anticipation, had suddenly been shortened and spoiled for him, but he had no complaint to make. He remained in his berth on the boat, beside his mother, until the return home.

This accident was a graphic example to those present of the value of cool self-control in perilous moments, and it served also to illustrate the uncalculated influence and result of the seed-sowing of wise practical thoughts, when dropped into the receptive soil of a young boy's mind.

IV.

"MORNING-GLORIES ARE IN BLOSSOM."

I CAN see him now, and hear that childish treble as it sought to bring these simple words, again and again repeated, within the meter of the song he had improvised for the occasion. I say improvised, but really it was a song of gladness gushing out of the fullness of his youthful heart. It was like the singing of a young bird just trying its first notes of exuberant joy at the gift of life.

Between the old stone church and the parsonage, at Alton, on the high bluffs overlooking the Mississippi, there was a narrow, shady space where, in summer days, we were wont to sit and catch the cool breezes always wandering by. Underneath a maple-tree was a wooden bench facing the house, and upon one end of this the boyish chorister had unpremeditatively taken his seat.   He must amuse himself, for his older brother and his mother were confined to their rooms by a mild sickness   Beneath the window some morning-glory seeds had been planted in the Springtime, and now, in August, the vines had begun to send forth their slowly-unfolding, tapering buds.

Arthur's sharp eyes had caught sight of a few of these buds which had suddenly burst into full bloom, and had gleefully brought the news to me, urging me to come and look at their delicate beauty.   Soon afterwards, as he still sat looking at the fragile blossoms, I heard him softly singing to himself: *"Morning-glories are in blossom! Morning-glories are in blossom!"*

Over and over went the refrain.   And as I stood at a chamber window, looking down at him as he spontaneously wafted this little musical poem out upon the currents of the joy and harmony of life which he saw and felt all about him that summer morning, I was entranced with admiration and love at the beautiful sight. Here were childish joy and innocence, peace and contentment, all combined in one moment of exultant life, while his feet and hands kept time to the melody of his tender voice.   He scarcely took his eyes from the pink-and-white blossoms swaying in the sweet-scented wind as he sent half-unconsciously that little chanson out of the heart of innocent and happy boyhood. He must have felt himself, in those moments, played upon by some tender, irrepressible impulse flowing out of the heart of the Divine Harmony which floated his being upon its bosom, and the joy of it all broke into utterance through his childish lips.

That little incident has been photographed upon my memory ever since with a distinctness which remains undimmed. The beauty of it all as a picture, and the touching melody of that glad refrain, I shall carry to my grave. What was the reason that it should thus impress itself so indelibly upon my consciousness? It must have been because it was a vivid revelation of the oneness of the child-heart with the beauty and joy of Nature; of the happiness which suffused his heart and over-ran its trembling brim because his life was in tune with the Infinite Life. I have heard fine music rendered by renowned artists; but I feel sure I would willingly do without them all to listen once again to that boyish voice as I heard it on that summer morning singing with an indescribably sweet and artless inspiration that little verse of exceeding joy at the goodness of life: "*Morning-glories are in blossom! Morning-glories are in blossom!*"

Dear little boy-caroller of that far away summer morning! You sang better than you knew, for you sang out of the heart of a divinely-beautiful love and joy and hope. Your song was not lost, for it went straight home to my heart, and will, continue to sing there forevermore. And here, in this page, I send it on its way, singing elsewhere and to others that same sweet, tender, impulsive refrain of joy at the goodness and happiness of life: "*Morning-glories are in blossom! Morning-glories are in blossom!*"

V.

"I LIVE FOR THOSE WHO LOVE ME."

I live for those who love me,
  Whose hearts are kind and true,
For the heaven that smiles above me
  And waits my spirit, too;
For the human ties that bind me,
For the task by God assigned me,
For the bright hours left behind me,
  And the good that I can do.

WHAT beautiful words for any child to love; what a noble ideal for any child to try to live! And *he* loved and lived these words. They are from a song with the same title, which Arthur learned from "The Carol," a Sunday-school service-book, one Winter spent in northern Wisconsin, when he was eleven years of age. Other songs he sang and liked, others may have spoken to him in more alluring music; but these words, and the music wedded to them, seemed

to have found a peculiar and permanent place
in his thought and affection, of which we did
not know at the time.   That he so dearly loved
this particular song was most touchingly revealed
to us during his last days, and so we came to
know then that he must have "hid it in his
heart" during all the intervening years.   And if
what we most deeply love reveals to us our true
characters, then his love for this little song
revealed his true character and the things in life
which to him were dearest and best.

It is with a sweetly sad pleasure that we now
try to picture to ourselves the first delicate
stirrings of tender emotion which came to his
sensitive heart-life, as he read and sang from
Sunday to Sunday these simple words of spiritual
confession,—"*I live for those who love me.*"
This affectionate ideal must have found a swift
response in the promptings of his unselfish
spirit, for his life was ever tuned to the same
key-note of the giving of himself for the welfare
of others.   Arthur could easily understand the
meaning of these words of simple heart-avowal,
and as an ideal of action and duty the song must
have appealed most persuasively to his spirit,
eagerly receptive of whatever was kind and

noble, pure and sweet. In connection with the simplicity of the song, the musical cadences, half sad, half pathetic, in which the words first sung themselves to him, seemed well fitted to carry so precious a thought straight home to the deepest feelings of so young and impressionable a boy. During all his life, Arthur did live "for those who loved him." To the divine harmony of this great and beautiful thought, he attuned his own life-work, and thence this loved song of his later years has become a part of the sweetest music of his memory.

To those, furthermore, "*whose hearts were kind and true,*" was he very naturally and sympathetically drawn; for in these he found spirits congenial with his own. And how subtle is the attraction between such kind and true natures! The being kind and the being true were the magnets which always drew his gentle spirit and held it obedient to its primal instinct of helpfulness to others. This impulse was very spontaneous in him.

"*For the human ties that bind me*" expresses simply another reason for his liking of this song; for he was very strongly attached to those bound to him by home or love ties. He felt

keenly and deeply the tender sanctities expressed
by the words "son" and "brother," and he
practised the sacred duties of the one as faith-
fully as he exercised the fraternal privileges of
the other.   He enjoyed the living of the life
made up of these tender human ties that bind
us so strongly together in the domesticities of
love and affection.

"And the task by God assigned me" he also
evidently believed in, for he lived by trust and
hope, always.   If he was to live, it would be
best; and if he was not to live, that, also, he
would accept as best.   He did not question —
he simply trusted.   His belief was that God had
given him something worth the doing, and he
did not either shrink from or expect to escape
that task.   He ever stood ready to do his part.

"The bright hours left behind me" was perhaps
to him a prophetic foresight of what his own life
should be to others when it was passed.   For,
brighter hours could no youth of sixteen years
leave behind him, to comfort bereaved hearts,
than did he.   These hours and days of his were
spent in such bright and sweet, such noble and
wholesome ways, that there can be no thought
of regret or sadness concerning them, now that

they have gone by and become a part of the irrevocable past. They are forever safe in precious memory,— the dower of a blessed spirit rich in youthful happiness and helpfulness.

"And the good that I can do." These were the words, in the song, summing up and condensing all in the lines foregoing which had called forth the love and admiration of the boy-singer. And all this was what it meant to him. It told of these blessed ways and opportunities for doing good, and doing good was what he loved to do above all things else — this was his life. Goodness is love in action; and to do good was his way of expressing his love to the little world about him. This was the gospel, the "good news," which he had loved from the beginning, and to the spreading of which he was earnestly glad to devote the brief days of his uncertain life. This little song was his Psalm of Life, treasured up and loved as the dearest he had ever known.

VI.

FLECKS OF SUNSHINE.

VERY happy were most of Arthur's days in Iowa. He was glad to get farther South again, for he loved plenty of sunshine, and his health required the warmer air. He had been very sick, and as soon as fairly well again he entered with quiet participation, but keen zest, into the new life of the new home. Here we built us a new house, and Arthur helped as he could. He carved in the foundation-stone the date of the beginning of work on the structure,— "May 12, 1893."

In this new locality of our residence, what a wealth of fresh things he did, delightful to a boy's heart! Among other things, there were many fishing-trips to the "Coon" river, and whether any "luck" rewarded his efforts, or not, the fun of the pastime was not lessened. It was the trying which was alluring; the testing of the unknown fish-life and possibilities hidden in the muddy waters along the banks.

There were horse-back rides on " Dandy," the old cream-colored pet horse of a neighbor,— a steed to whom it mattered little whether one, two, or three, mounted his back at one time and enjoyed the fun. What boy, older grown, would not envy these children the delicious sensation of their first horse-back rides — the moving, swaying and clinging to the horse's back as the great body of warm flesh cantered or walked whither the fickle wills of the motley band of youngsters directed.

Or, it was a ride in the buggy with the same " Dandy " as motive-power, and with the boys and girls scattered about in all possible situations of youthful unrest and enjoyment. To a boy, what is more enticing than to be able to journey where one pleases by the mere pulling of a leather string, with a " cluck " to the old horse! What boyish experience could seem more delightfully satisfying,— this freedom of action, this novelty of enjoyment, such as a boy of twelve can know only once in his life!

Sometimes the boys went over to "Beaver Creek" timber-land, to hold a "strictly private" picnic,— taking along with them lunch-baskets and fishing-tackle, and the keenest of appetites both for fun and food. Of course, the first duty would be to examine the contents of their baskets; for what healthy boy or girl is not hungry as soon as arrived on a picnic-ground? Then there would be the gathering of wild-flowers, and of curiosities of vegetation or rock; the swinging on wild grape-vines, the wading in shallow water, the hunting of bird's-nests for "one egg" for collection purposes, and all the various other odds and ends of enjoyment to be had in Springtime in the woods.

"Not much to make us happy
Do any of us need,
But just the right thing give us
And we are rich indeed."

In this way the merry campaigns for simple fun and out-door enjoyment went on each summer and winter season.

The gathering of several albums of postage-stamps at this time afforded the boys much pleasure, and gave them considerable business-correspondence as well as lessons in geography and current history. How they traded and "dickered" in these little bits of colored and pictured paper, a great deal as men enjoy the gathering and exchanging of bank-bills, — all children together. Very real and full of interest was this phase of his experience to Arthur. He kept his collections with care, and hours of innocent happiness came to him from this "playing at business." Moreover, it was as educative to him as is the doing of all things we enjoy, whether we call it work or play.

It was while living here that Arthur bought and learned to play his first harmonica. His first efforts in this line were, to be sure, rather discouraging; but in a few weeks he could render easily various home and Sunday-school songs. Afterwards, he became quite an adept in its use, and could readily produce on this instrument any song or tune he had heard. One of my best remembered profile pictures of Arthur represents him at this and later times playing his harmonica with quiet enjoyment, beating time with his foot. This occupation brought to his music-hungry heart those simple strains of melody which he loved best,— songs of tenderest feeling, others suggestive of home scenes and happiness. If the inventor of this little instrument could know of the many hours of real soul-enjoyment he has given to the years of boyhood, he would feel that he had not been an insignificant agent in producing that youthful happiness which is a part of the music of the world.

One incident of the life in Iowa illustrates afresh Arthur's habitual calmness and self-possession; and it came in a way to test any boy's courage and presence of mind. One summer evening, we had left Arthur at a friend's house, playing with children both larger and smaller than himself, while we went to a sociable on the opposite side of the village. The sky was threatening, and, before we arrived at our destination, a small cyclone suddenly rose towards the west and swept down through the streets of Perry. The air was full of dust, and of the sound of loosening boards and shutters. Everyone sought shelter. At the house where Arthur was staying, some one had already spread the news that the telegraph had given warning of the approach of a cyclone; and, in Iowa, this is a much dreaded piece of news. Naturally, when the fierce wind-storm mentioned darkened

the sky and threatened to bring destruction, the
people in the neighborhood were alarmed, and
all of the children had run hastily into the
house, frantic with fear. "Grandpa" Willis
stood in their midst, trying to quiet them, while
they cried, trembled, shouted, and ran about in
a half-frenzied manner — all except Arthur, who
stood cool and undisturbed among them, seem-
ing to have no fear for himself, and thinking
and speaking only of the possible danger to his
father and mother.

His example of calm courage quieted the
other children. The storm passed away without serious injury to any one.

Between these flecks of sunshine came some
dark days. Another attack of the rheumatism
upon Arthur, while living here, brought renewed
anxiety to our hearts. It was Winter, and for
weeks he had withstood the pain hopefully and
uncomplainingly. At last the pain reached his
heart, and he was troubled to get his breath.
He was obliged to sit with his arms thrown
over the pillow in front of him.

It was while thus clinging to life for days, with his fortitude and patience nearly exhausted, that he turned on one occasion to his mother, who stood beside him, and said: "Mamma, I don't think I can hold on any longer."

Life at such frequent times was so hard a struggle for him; it was so very painful and serious in comparison with his little enjoyment in it; there was so much sickness between his short experiences of health, that at times he was ready and willing to give it all up. And still he hoped.

Once there came a strange experience. Arthur and I often shared the same bed, if he was feeling badly. We had retired one night, and lay for some time talking of various things, when gradually our talk drifted to some experiences of his past life, to his frequent sicknesses, and, in some way, dying was referred to. He seemed to be feeling unusually serious, and, I thought, agitated by something that troubled his mind. I therefore finally said:

"What is it, Arthur? Is there something that troubles you — something that you wish to tell me?"

Then he broke forth with such earnestness of

speech that I was startled, as he tremblingly sobbed out these words, clinging to my neck:

"Papa, I hope you won't die before I do."

I was deeply touched, and tried to soothe his agitated thoughts by assuring him, as best I could, that he would always have some one to care for him whenever he was sick or in trouble. It was anxiety concerning this which troubled him. He knew that I understood his needs, and that he could always feel sure, while I lived, of that sympathy and love which his soul craved to have expressed.

What a pathetic and prophetically prayerful wish was this, for so young a boy to make! He was willing to go first, and preferred it to remaining behind alone, because he might not always meet with those "whose hearts were kind and true," those whom he could love, and to help whom he would wish to live.

At one time we were obliged to be absent from home for two nights, and we left Arthur in the care of friends, where there were children with whom he could play. This was his first experi-

ence of absence from his parents for the length
of time stated, yet he seemed willing to have us
go.   When we returned, he met us at the train,
and seemed very glad to see us, yet he made no
confession of the great test of his courage our
absence had required.   Just *how glad* he was
to see us we never knew for a long time afterward.   When the news of his death, later on,
reached this friend with whom Arthur had
stayed, she sent us a consoling letter, in which
were these pathetic words :

" We were pained and surprised on hearing of
the death of our little friend Arthur, whom we
all loved and admired for his manly little ways
and happy disposition.   I think none of us will
soon forget the day or two he spent with us;
how happy he seemed by day, and how he
mourned at night for his father and mother.
And I can imagine that his only sorrow, in leaving off this life for the brighter one, may be
that of your loneliness and grief."

This was a painfully sad reference to an
experience at the time unknown to us, showing
the same uncomplaining self-forgetfulness in
connection with those he loved, however much
he himself might suffer.   "How he mourned at

night for his father and mother" tells it all. These words, coming to us when they did, seemed like the sweetly sad strains of some dear music which we had heard in the past and had forgotten, until we heard it again.

Following this, came the ever-memorable ten days which all of us spent at the World's Fair in Chicago. On the trip to the city we stopped for a few weeks with friends at "Plowman Heights," on Rock River, near its entrance into the Mississippi. Here we found an ideal summer-resort, and passed days of idyllic pleasure on the hillside, among the trees. To the boys concerned it was an especially attractive and happy experience. It was, in fact, as near a Boy's Paradise as is possible to be realized. What with rides bare-back on the Shetland ponies, and with them harnessed in gigs, the fishing out of all waters within easy reach, the waking up in the morning to see flying-squirrels running overhead, the finding afterwards of their nesting-place in the split trunk of a tree, the sleeping in tents out of doors, the blackberrying and water-melon experiences, and the farewell bonfire on top of the hill just before leaving; — these and other scenes and experiences have left sweetest memories of the happy days we all spent here in the company of congenial friends, including many boys, and make one of the brightest pictures upon which we can look as we turn the kaleidoscope of memory's varied treasures. Here Arthur was merry and happy.

VII.

"BOYS AND GIRLS TOGETHER."

So nigh is grandeur to our dust,
  So near is God to man,
When Duty whispers low, *Thou must,*
  The youth replies, *I can.*
                              —*Emerson.*

AFTER living in the West for many years, it seemed best to come East, for the better education of our boys, for the new environments it would bring to us, and with the hope that the change might prove beneficial to Arthur.

And during the first year of our residence in Massachusetts, his health greatly improved, and we were much encouraged, feeling that perhaps the critical point had been passed, and that he was now to outgrow the past weaknesses and tendencies implanted by the scarlet-fever of his early childhood. It was a year which he enjoyed very much, for it was full of change, of novel

(47)

incident, and of new situations of peculiar interest to his maturing boyhood.

On coming to Whitman, Arthur entered the Grammar School at once, and was soon promoted. This pleased him exceedingly, for it meant entrance into the High School the next year — an ambition which had been deferred owing to his enforced absence from school on account of his frequent ill-health.

The pupils here were taught many things not usually included in school courses, namely: to observe the changes of the seasons, to look for the date of arrival of the first birds in Spring, of the first buds to open, and the first wild-flowers to appear. There were various short excursions into the country, collecting stones and minerals. Specimens of woods were obtained and labeled. And thus, as a whole, the love for Nature-study was called forth and gratified, at the same time that the mind was being disciplined in thought-studies.

Into all these features of his school work and life, Arthur entered with unusual interest, for it meant out-door exercise, the free enjoyment of Nature, the satisfaction of his love for beautiful and interesting things. It meant especially the formation at home of a cabinet-collection of the specimens secured. It meant also the Saturday holidays, with the rides on his bicycle to neighboring ponds, woods and rural resorts, in which often a small company of boys and girls, school-companions, would join. This was varied by a hunting-trip in Winter, by many fishing-trips in Spring, bicycle-rides to near-by ponds for bathing and swimming, the gathering of Mayflowers and other wild beauties of the woods, while in Summer there was the picking of blueberries, and picnic-trips to Nantasket and other resorts. He had, as associates, two boys of about his own age, and with them he spent many happy hours, studying and playing with them, trading stamps, working an electric battery,—all in the closest and freest intimacy of happy, fresh and disinterested boyhood.

It could hardly have been a happier experience, this of young school boys and girls together; and I never pass by the school-house without thinking of his happy days in it, and of my several visits to his room. I can see him in memory still, studying at his desk or rising to recite with that quiet modesty so characteristic of him.

There was a little verse he had learned, which he often repeated at home:

> "Build a little fence of trust
>   Around to-day;
> Fill the space with loving words,
>   And therein stay."

And he did this spontaneously and habitually, living in the atmosphere of trust and cheer created at home by his own loving words and kindness of manner.

Late in the spring term, there came to town a traveling photographer. Offering small tin-types at a minimum price, he secured the patronage of all the scholars. Arthur sat twice, and this proved one of those sadly fortunate little things which, looked back upon afterwards, seemed providential, for otherwise we should have had no late picture of him.

Arthur arranged his "exchange" collection of tiny portraits in a group, on a large piece of card-board, with himself and his particular "chum" in the center, writing underneath:

> "*Boys and Girls Together: Eighth Grade,*
>   1895–6."

This showed his care and foresight, however unavailing; for his idea evidently was that these pictures of his schoolmates, thus arranged, he could look upon with happy and tender recollections in future years. Ah! the sad sweetness of these little things done by children, in such implicit anticipation of future pleasure! In this, how much they are like ourselves — they with their toys of a day, and we with ours!

Then came his happy summer vacation; first, with three weeks spent at the "No Name" cottage at the sea-side, his and our first experience of close contact with the ocean. This was followed by a few weeks quietly enjoyed at home, ending with a short trip alone to Vermont, to visit cousins whom he had not seen for five years.

It surprised him to find that we thought he could make this trip by himself, but he was ready for it. He made all the preparations with his usual care, including a fishing outfit, and went off on the cars. The picture is with me yet,— of his sitting at the car-window with his white cap on, and smiling and waving his hand in farewell. So happy, oh, so happy!

He mailed us a postal-card on reaching the station where his journey by rail ended, and then walked four miles, three of which were up hill,— a good woman on the way giving him a bowl of brown-bread and milk during a shower which overtook him.

Gladsome, joyous days on the Vermont hillside then followed, in which he breathed the tonic air and enjoyed the luxury of exultant life with every thought and motion. To this, add affectionate cousins, a table abundantly fitted to satisfy hungry appetites three times a day, and play-days all the time — was not this a boy's own land of Constant Delight?

But these were too short and happy days to last, and the first of September found Arthur in Whitman again, ready and eager to enter the High School. This entrance was to be the gratification of the fond ambition of his later boyhood years. He had learned, by reason of the uncertainty of his health, to hold all his plans and wishes in abeyance; but at last this great desire was to be fulfilled.

Always very conscientious in preparing his lessons, he now took up his new school duties with the same sense of faithfulness. He became a favorite with his schoolmates, and enjoyed keenly this new school-life of "boys and girls together."

Arthur had a quiet and quick sense of the humorous things in life, and from this gift he got many happy compensations for the losses resulting from his deprivations. He gathered clippings of comic pictures and verses, queer sayings and jokes, and placed them in a scrap-book, entitled, "Book of Poems and Verses." He was also very facile and suggestive in the use of his pencil, and could easily draw free hand. This gift was often exercised in humorous scenes and situations, depicting some exaggerated personal peculiarity in those he met. He drew also birds, plants and flowers. His faculty of inventing unique and artistic variations of capital text-letters promised something for future cultivation and use. His limited correspondence was always a pleasure to him, being conducted with great care, and with a maturity of expression unusual for one of his years.

During a few months at this time he "carried papers," and gave to its conduct the same faithfulness and system that he exhibited in all

things in which he engaged. He earned money
enough out of this occupation to pay for a suit
of clothes for himself, proudly showing me the
receipt for the same when paid for.

❧

But Arthur's period of good-health gradually
began to lessen its promise of permanent
stability. There was a subtle and slow deteriora-
tion of physical strength and vitality. His
studies became more burdensome to him, one
was dropped, and his teachers were requested to
lighten the demands made upon him. In the
Winter we wished him to drop out of school for
a while, until he might recover greater strength:
but he could not think now of giving up his
studies at the High School. He had been sick
so often before, and had recovered his health
so many times,— why could he not do the same
now? And so the winter months went by, in
anxiety, and yet in hope of his improvement
with the coming of Spring.

Things were done to cheer him, and to give his
mind diversion. In late Winter a Baby Hawkeye
Kodak was bought, and this afforded him much

pleasure.   He himself fitted up a "dark-room,"
and began to take and develop pictures, the
printing of which he attended to on sunshiny
afternoons.   He also spent some spare hours in
fixing up a small chamber which was to be "his
room."   Here he gathered together all his curios
and relics and coins, and carefully arranged them
in a small cabinet he himself had made.   The
walls of this room of his were decorated with
favorite pictures, and with various artistic designs
conceived and arranged by himself.   All this gave
him diversion and pleasure, and he continued
making his plans for the future in his usual
painstaking, cheerful way.

But finally, in March, it became evident to
him as well as to us that his school-duties were
too exacting for one in his debilitated condition,
and that he needed an entire release from study
and work.   At the spring vacation, therefore, he
left the High School and remained at home, to
renew if he might his health and strength.   His
teachers and school-friends called to see and
encourage him, bringing fruit and flowers.   He
took short walks and was given carriage-rides
that he might have the benefit of the open air.
At times he felt strong enough even to mount

and ride away on his wheel for short distances. But all these exercises became less and less frequent, and in early May, with the Spring in its most inviting aspect, he was obliged to take to his bed.

Sad and seemingly unnatural experience! — this lying down of a youth upon a sick-bed from which he is never to arise, and upon which at length he is to breathe out his last fluttering breath !

VIII.

GOING TO VERMONT.

ARTHUR did not seem to improve with the advance of the Spring, as we had hoped he would, and so we began to plan for a change of surroundings for him. Various suggestions were considered, but, as a final result of our consultations, strengthened by the advice of the physician, it was thought best to try again the restorative power of the Vermont air and sunshine and higher altitudes.

He was to go as soon as arrangements could be made, and his strength was sufficient for the journey. But delays came in, to postpone; and his strength became yet more uncertain. The days and weeks of May and of early June thus found him still waiting to go, and with the date not yet fixed.

But the happiness of those last days to him

was in *hoping to go*, and in planning all the little details of the looked-for trip. How joyfully he anticipated the pleasures of the proposed change, and how thoughtfully he planned for its execution! At such times, the sweetest of tender smiles would shine upon his face, as he would suggest the many things he could do, up in "dear old Vermont"; and then his large, dreamy eyes would be filled with that look of happy content which comes to children easily pleased with the prospect of gratifying their heart's fairest desire. He spoke of a kodak he wished to take along; of the good times he was sure would be possible fishing for brook-trout on Uncle Austin's farm; and of all the joys of the previous Summer's experience, which he hoped to be able to duplicate, or even exceed, when once more upon the farm.

It was this hope and expectancy which buoyed him up to his normal attitude of cheer and trust. He was so anxious to go that he could talk of little else. Time-tables were consulted, and a special one for his own use prepared on a piece of card-board; letters were written, and all contingencies provided for. We had no serious doubt that it would not be possible for him to go, and our expectation cheered his own strong desire into implicit belief. "Dear old Vermont," where is such air and water, grass and sunshine, as nowhere else, seemed the ideal place in which to recover his health. And then the fun, the sports, the romps and plays on the farm, the little out-door lunches and trips into the woods,— how entrancing all these visions seemed, luring and tempting the boy's mind, so hungry for the innocent pleasures of youthful life, he being now just at the age when he was best ready to enjoy these to the uttermost!

Oh, if he could only be well once more! He loved to talk of it, over and over again, and dwelt with especial happiness on the enjoyment of fishing in and playing about a certain brook of clearest water, which ran gurgling, rippling and winding through woods and meadow, and was filled with the little "speckled beauties," the catching of which so tempts and calls forth a boy's skill.

Talking about the brook was not enough to satisfy his craving for the deferred enjoyment of a drink from its brim. One day he wished to have a large saucer, filled with cold water, brought to him, so that he could play "drinking out of the brook." Lying upon one side, and placing his lips in the water, he quickly drew it

up with that peculiar sucking sound suggestive
of brook-drinking when one's thirst leads to this
primitive method of satisfaction. This "playing" at the real brook-drinking which he had so
often practised in Vermont helped to keep up
the illusion which always goes before the realization of happiness,— an illusion which, to all
youthful minds, is so delightful to indulge in.
But, the pathos of that touching incident, as it
now rises before me! The hungry, wistful look
in his face, as he played thus with the fond
fancies which filled his boyish heart; as he
sought to make these once again real by the
childish power of suggestion — this forms one
of those fadeless pictures which belong to the
sacredness of parental experience.

When we recall how little it takes, usually, to
satisfy a child's love for happiness, how do the
frequent denials and deprivations of childhood
rise up to condemn us! Boys and girls belong
to the out-door life of free Nature, and the primal
enjoyments should be theirs with an unstinted
freedom.

❧

The day at last had been set on which the
journey to Vermont was to be made. And as

the time was only a few days away, the decision filled the boy's heart to the brim with the joy of expectation.

He was soon to be sixteen years of age; and he said, how fine it would be to spend his sixteenth birthday with his cousins on the loved Vermont hillside farm !

Each day was busy with the necessary preparations, and his eyes glowed with a deep sense of satisfaction that the start was so near at hand.

The forenoon of his last day was busily spent in getting all the details of his little affairs into good shape, even to the writing of a postal-card after dinner. And then ——

🌑

What strangely tender thoughtfulness of the Great Kindness, that all this should be done, and our eyes be shaded thus far, so that we could not see the end so near at hand ! The journey to Vermont was not to be undertaken, and what had taken place revealed to us why it was not best. The beautiful and delicate physical casket could no longer retain the jewel of such heavenly love and tenderness. The dear boy, who so longed to go up among the Green Hills and spend his Summer there, was gently, and, oh, so kindly led, without pain, and with suspended consciousness, on, and on, towards the New Land of strange delights, until, as the evening shadows fell, he was peacefully ushered into the valleys of the Celestial Vermont, and his beautiful feet rested upon the hills that are forever green.

Upon that eagerly-looked-forward-to sixteenth birthday of his, we laid his beautiful form away in the cool, dry bosom of mother-earth, in a sunny spot, in sight of and in nearness to his own last-known earthly home, his church, his high-school, and to the park and pond and roads with which he was so familiar. Only a week before his passing away, he had taken his last ride, and passed by this very spot where his weary body was to find sweet repose.

The beautiful ripe June day was not more beautiful than was this earthly casket in which had dwelt, for sixteen years, so sweet, pure and holy a spirit. Under the shady branches of a young oak-tree we took our farewell look of the Divine Boy whom God had sent to bless our lives and the little world in which he lived.

PART II.

SADNESS AND GLADNESS.

Out of the day and night
A joy has taken flight.

—*Shelley.*

And looking over the hills, I mourn
The darling who shall not return.

—*Emerson's "Threnody."*

Nor time, nor space, nor deep, nor high,
Can keep my own away from me.

—*John Burroughs.*

Now I can love thee truly,
For nothing comes between
The senses and the spirit,
The seen and the unseen.

—*Lowell.*

Grief should be
Like joy, majestic, equable, sedate;
Confirming, cleansing, raising, making free,
Strong to consume small troubles; to command
Great thoughts, grave thoughts, thoughts lasting to
the end.   —*Aubrey de Vere.*

Of perfect service rendered, duties done
In charity, soft speech and stainless days:
These riches shall not fade away in life,
Nor any death dispraise.

—*Sir Edwin Arnold.*

(64)

PART II.

SADNESS AND GLADNESS.

IX.

THROUGH TEARS OF MEMORY.

Some of the incidents and scenes of those last weeks stand forth in memory with that clear-cut distinctness which loving affection alone can outline and preserve. The tenderness of these seemed unusually touching at the time, but the coming of the Shadow has now made them doubly pathetic and precious; and as we recall them in the present we see them through the tears of memory,— little pictures of the heart's remembrance which are unforgettable.

During the last weeks Arthur became, by reason of his steady decline and increasing weakness, even more strikingly child-like than was his habitual manner. It seemed as if he had again returned to his childhood years; his voice and manner of speech became even more gentle and subdued.

It was at this time that we first learned of his special affection for the touching song in "The Carol," before referred to,—"I live for those who love me." One day I was trying to sing it, from memory rather than from sight, though I had nearly forgotten it. I did not succeed very well, and Arthur, hearing, called to me to bring the book to him and he would show me how it should be sung. I can see now the smiling eagerness with which he took the book, and with a weakened, trembling voice began to sing forth the beautiful words to that half-sad melody. He sang it through, and very correctly, and then said to me:

"Do you know, papa, that is my favorite song: the one I love best?"

Its beautiful application to his own life, and the memory of the above tenderly pathetic recital of it, has made a place for it in our memories, very precious and indelible. And since it was sung at the home-service of final farewell as we sat looking upon his peaceful face, this little heart-song of his special love can never be to us other than sacred music — it has been dedicated to his memory forever.

One of his most habitual means of expressing his happiness,— indicative of his hopeful disposition,— was by singing, the playing of his harmonica, or by whistling. Among his favorite songs were "Home, Sweet Home," "The Old Oaken Bucket," "Sunlight in my Soul," with various medleys of a lively or humorous character. His voice was naturally strong and clear, and its sweetness never more discernible than when singing. And yet perhaps his most characteristic enjoyment of music was in whistling the songs, tunes and hymns which he had learned and liked. Into this simple exercise seemed to go all the melody of his heart-life, all the cheerfulness and hopefulness of his nature. A happy-hearted, whistling boy — what more joyous sight or sound! One of the tenderest recollections of Arthur which comes to us is that of this spontaneous bubbling over of his happiness at the simple fact of being alive.

We most easily associate it with his home-coming in the twilight. Often when he had gone out to spend the afternoon with some boy-

friend, as he started to return and drew near
home he would begin whistling, and in such
clear and exultant tones that we could hear and
recognize it while he was yet far away. It was
always unmistakable in its joyous tone of simple
happiness — the sweet, warbling songs of this
cheerful-hearted boy coming home at night-fall
to those he loved! Ah, those moments of delicate
enjoyment, which the tendrils of a sacred asso-
ciation hold so preciously intertwined in the
memory, so that whenever is now heard by us
the happy whistle of a boy passing near the
house in the twilight, we, remembering, look up
and into each other's faces, and see the hope,
quickly sprung up there, as suddenly die down!

On the 13th of May occurred his mother's
birthday. A joint contribution from the other
members of the family had obtained for her a
gold pen and pearl holder, and it was suggested
that Arthur be allowed in the evening to do the
surprising in a little speech of presentation. As
the time arrived, he remained quiet a few minutes, rehearsing the thoughts and words of it to

himself. Then he said he was ready, and with
a pleased smile he recited it to me beforehand.
Soon she was called into the room and made to
know that Arthur wished to say something to
her. With the little package in his hands, and
a tender smile flitting over his face, he held out
the little gift towards her, and said, in his soft-
est, gentlest tones : —"In behalf of the members
of this family, and in remembrance of this day,
I hereby present you this token of our love."

All our voices trembled a little, then, and the
tears came, too. Arthur was happiest of all, for
the gift was in exact keeping with his practice
for many years. He was habitually thoughtful
concerning the getting of gifts for the members
of the family at the holidays and upon our
several birthdays, always remembering these
latter recurrences with some little token of
remembrance made by his own hands. Into
these went his exuberant, never-ceasing love for
others. His heart's fondest longing was thus
satisfied; for

> "It is only love that can give,
> It is only by loving we live."

Arthur's love for flowers was in harmony with his fondness for all things beautiful, sweet and good. On several occasions he had gone on trips to gather the early wild "Mayflowers" (*Arbutus*). Making them into little bouquets, he had remembered his friends with them. In the yard, under the horse-chestnut tree, grew large quantities of the early blue violets called "Johnny-jump-ups." He spent many hours among these, and could not let any child go away empty handed. He saw the first grass crocus springing up by the door-step, and watched for the first opening of each bud and blossom. On the last Sunday morning of his life, a wedding took place at our house, and the groom, learning of Arthur's serious and long sickness, sent in to him several of the beautiful white roses which the bride had held. This pleased Arthur much. They were placed beside his bed, where he could look at them and enjoy their fragrance; and there they remained, feeding his hunger for earthly beauty, until his eyes turned at length to feast themselves upon the loveliness of the flowers of heaven.

A few days before he passed on, the trellised red roses in the yard began to open their buds, and Arthur, sitting raised up in bed one morning, was the first to see them through the window, and called my attention to them. It was his habit, after having his face and hands washed and his hair brushed, to lean back against the piled-up pillows. It all comes back to me now like a picture,— a silhouette in my memory: his mother's light red shawl thrown about his shoulders, his hands folded helplessly, child-like, across his breast, his face turned appealingly towards the window, looking out of it in silence so longingly at the roses, at the foliage, and all the greenery outside!

Of what was he thinking?

X.

THINGS SWEET TO REMEMBER.

"FOLD closer and closer in your hearts his sunshine. That was his life. A blessed spirit of divine love; and no flaw was in him; and he is yours."

So wrote his aunt, after he had passed on. And that is the sweetest comfort that comes to our hearts, as we think it all over for the thousandth time. To feel reassured beyond possible doubt that, when Arthur left us, he left no sting of remorse behind, no sore, aching sense of regret, no wearying heart-ache for anything done by him in all his earthly life,— this was a rare blessing vouchsafed to us. He lived in such kindly sympathy with all beautiful, true and good things that, when he was done with them, no one could openly or silently lift up hands of reproach against his memory. This blessed consciousness, these hallowed recollections, are now ours, and they sweeten and comfort our sorrow as can nothing else. They are the things sweetest to remember. We love often to think about these, and to speak of them to each other,— of his youthful graces of character and goodnesses of heart, for these have now become the fairest rosary in our memories, told over again and again.

Perhaps the most beautiful and attractive feature of his disposition was his unfailing thoughtfulness for others. This meant sympathy for everybody, the putting of himself in their places. He was always ready and willing to set aside his own wishes or desires to please somebody else. So tender was his heart, so finely attuned to the joy or suffering of others, that it could not refuse the simplest appeal for help or sympathy. He was not only happy when others were happy, but he suffered when others were unhappy. He had known already, in his brief life, much of pain and sickness and disappointment; and so he could and did most quickly and keenly enter into the sufferings, the troubles and losses of others. In our household life he always exhibited a peculiar sensitiveness to any personal need or distress. Had his mother been working very hard ? He seemed in some quickly instinctive way to know it, and his invariable question was: "Are you tired, mamma ?" or, "Can I help you, mamma ?" And then would follow quietly the earnest attempt to lighten the burden. It might be some necessary detail of housework, like his habitual wiping of the dishes, sometimes sweeping the floor, or making his bed, bringing in wood, going to the grocery-store, or other errand or task. Whatever it was, he was anxious and instantly ready to do the thing needing to be done. If his mother was sick, there was the quick response in gentle touch and soothing voice and tender manner. All his playthings had to wait, all the little plans and projects dear to his boy-heart were held in abeyance, until the little acts of helpfulness were done. These home needs and duties so appealed to his sympathy that they were not to be neglected or postponed. In the same way, his spirit of helpfulness flowed forth to help all who were tired, or sick, or in trouble.

Another thing sweet to remember was his spontaneous kindness of disposition and conduct in general. It greeted you like a delicate fragrance as you came into his presence. When he was at hand, all felt it; when he was absent, all seemed to miss it. Stored up in his throbbing little breast was a wealth of good will and tenderness for every one and every thing. He never knew what malice meant; there was no resentment whatever in his nature. Others might attack him, or speak slightingly of him (as boys sometimes will of each other), and yet it never seemed to rankle in his memory or ruffle the peaceful repose of his disposition. And this was not weakness, either; none knew better than he how he was being treated; but his idea seemed to be, even though he may never have formulated it in so many words, that "nobleness enkindleth nobleness." This quality of his character was especially noticeable and attractive. Free from all ill will himself, he carried no cruel shafts of sharply-spoken words about with him to wound his friends or playmates. He never lent himself to the low enjoyment of playing tricks upon others; never tormented dogs or cats or other animals, or took pleasure in any form of cruelty. Always he sought to show kindness to every little creature, and by words and actions helped to preach and spread the gospel of kindness.

For this reason his presence was always agreeable and sought after, and his companionship enjoyable. His whole demeanor and influence spoke for peace, kindness and boy-like honor, and so he was a favorite at social gatherings, on the play-ground, and upon excursions. Very pronounced, also, was his disinclination to enter into any inharmonious discussion or dispute. This avoidance of ill will, of angry feelings, and of personal dissensions, was habitual with him; indeed, he scarcely ever violated the ideal of peaceable behavior which he had adopted for his own. This eloquent attitude of silence on his part, this holding aloof from all excitement of controversy, was always felt as a rebuke — it was an example that was alive with meaning; it was like oil poured upon troubled waters.

> "Kind words can never die;
>   Cherished and blest,
> God knows how deep they lie
>   Stored in the breast.
> Like childhood's simple rhymes,
>   Said o'er a thousand times,
> They, in all years and climes,
>   Strengthen and cheer."

Arthur loved whatsoever was of good report. This is sweet to recall of him. Purity of thought and word and action was innate, instinctive, with him. Most rarely did an unworthy word linger upon his lips, and no sensual thought seemed to have stained the white radiance of his innocence. To look into his clear eyes was to see reflected there the honest, ingenuous thoughts of a pure-minded boy. Upon the palace-walls of his mind there were hung beautiful pictures of all things sweet and good which he had ever known. All things bright and fair were his by the magnetism of spiritual likeness — the one drew the other. Nowhere did he seem more in place than among the flowers which he so dearly loved. He was a part of the purity of the world.

A deep, abiding sense of loyalty to his parents is also one of the fairest things to remember in Arthur's life. When present, this is always a touching characteristic in children, for it reveals to the parents that ideal of themselves which their children hold with immovable trust and unsuspecting faith. The experience of it is always pathetic, since the child idealizes the real parent. In this idealization lies the pathos of it to fathers and mothers sensible of their imperfections. Arthur's loyalty was unquestioning in its child-like devotion and generous appreciation. He so loved his parents, and so wished them to love him in return, that obedience was never a hard or irksome thing for him, never a trial or an unhappy experience. Rather, it seemed always to be regarded by him as the most natural thing in the world, and as giving him a glad chance to do something to show his real filial affection. Usually no urging was necessary; to know our wishes was enough. He seemed anxious, indeed, to do the thing we wished him to do. His obedience was as natural and spontaneous as was his loving, and the one grew out of the other. It was voluntary, and full of the joyful spirit of his best impulses and highest gratifications. This meant a high sense of loyalty; for boy-nature is naturally self-assertive and inclined to be greatly wrapped up in its selfhood — in meeting its own many petty wants, its ever-changing, never-satisfied desires. Obedience to Arthur meant what it should mean to all boys — the setting aside for the time being, when necessary, of some of his own personal plans and cherished schemes for boyish pleasure. It meant

to him self-restraint, a thoughtfulness of what
was due to others,.the. reasonable subjection of
the boy-will to the parental will,—and yet all in
such a cheerful, hearty manner that it was really
a harmony of wills and brought in the end an
enjoyment all the keener and more satisfying.

His joyful, loving obedience, the implicit,
whole-souled loyalty of his nature to whatever
was right and just as we commended these to
him, becomes for us one of the most gracious
memories of his life, "sweetening and gathering
sweetness forever more."

With the coming of the lonely, hushed days
after the last sad services had been rendered,
there came letters from kinsfolk and friends.
Sweet indeed is the memory of these messages,
fragrant from the hands of a sincere love and
affection. How precious they were in those
hours of freshly-made sorrow, when we felt so
stricken and bereft; how they fed the hunger
for familiar human presence, and assuaged the
grief that could not be changed, letting us feel
the heart-beat of a tender sympathy common to

all who know such sorrow. These letters took us by the hand with tender pressure, lifted up our heads, and, looking as it were into our faces, showed us, present with others, the same grief that was ours. This one told of a memory, that one of a heart-ache, another gave comforting assurance of feelings "too deep for tears," while yet another uttered her heart's confession of gratefulness for the beautiful life she had known. Precious letters,— they have helped, and their memory lies hid among our heart's treasures.

XI.

THE STORY OF THE DRAGON-FLY.

Yet Love will dream, and Faith will trust
(Since He who knows our need is just),
That somehow, somewhere, meet we must.
— *Whittier.*

I<small>T</small> was during Arthur's last illness that he told his mother "the Story of the Dragon-Fly," which he had remembered for three years. We cannot recall that he had ever spoken of it before, but he evidently had treasured it up as one of the things sweet to think about, and in which he believed with all the touching faith of a child's nature. He must have thought of its meaning many times, for this meaning had evidently become his most earnest personal conviction about the future life.

The telling of it, and his own confession of faith, came about in a very natural and beautiful

way. A mother had called one evening to tell
us of the death of her daughter, who had been
married only a few months. Arthur, in the
adjoining room, had heard the sad news and the
conversation which followed; and soon afterward
his mother, preparing him for his night's rest,
made ready herself to sleep beside him, as was
her practice. Their talk during this time drifted
naturally to the subject of dying; and, for the
first and only time, Arthur then seemed to be
in a mood to speak about this.

After a thoughtful silence, he suddenly asked
his mother if she remembered a certain story
which his father had once told about living
again after death? Arthur called it "the Story
of the Dragon-Fly," but the real title of it is,
"Not Lost, but Gone Before." It is a beautiful
Nature-analogy, written by Mrs. Gatty in suggestive illustration of the possibility of continued
existence beyond the change called death. It
had been quoted in a sermon delivered in Iowa
three years previously, at an Easter Commemo-
ration-service in which both church and Sunday-
school joined. Arthur was present, being then
nearly thirteen years of age, and it seemingly
made a great impression upon his youthful

imagination. He remembered the main facts in the story, and narrated them simply to his mother, to refresh her memory:

There was once a beautiful wood-pond, in the lower depths of which the grubs of dragon-flies lived. They fell to talking one day about what became of the frogs who rose to the top of the water and disappeared. The frogs, in response, tried to give them some information about the kind of world it was into which they rose, but it was very unsatisfactory. Finally, one of the grubs became sick, and, feeling that some change was coming, it climbed up the rush-stalks and disappeared from the sight of those left below. This caused great excitement and wonder among the other grubs, and promises were exacted and given among them that whenever the time came for the next grub to go in the same way, he would return and tell his mates what that upper world was like. Others soon disappeared, but none of them ever returned to tell what kind of a world it was to which they had gone. All agreed as to the irresistible desire to go which urged their fellows to rise to the surface, but none could explain the mystery of the failure to return. Yet this was easy to explain if the opportunity had been possible. The dragon-flies, into which the grubs had changed when they disappeared, had not forgotten their friends left behind nor their promises to return; but they had found, when they arrived in that other world, that they could not, with the new and different bodies which they then possessed, return again into the watery depths. They could only flit very lightly and happily over the surface of the water above, with their beautiful wings and shining bodies, and look down lovingly and longingly at their grub-mates below in their old haunts. The dragon-flies themselves knew all about the conditions of their fresh, happier life, but they could not carry or tell this knowledge to their grub-friends, nor could the grubs see or hear them. They had made a promise which they could not keep. They knew that their grub-friends would all come sometime to live the life of a free-soaring dragon-fly, but never could a dragon-fly return to his former life, or tell his former friends of the new and beautiful exist-ence he was then living. Each fresh arrival from below made those above happier, and happy was each new comer to find, not a strange and

friendless place, but a beautiful and attractive
home filled with the friends gone before.   Oh,
if those below could only know!   But all they
could do was to live in hope and trust of a
reunion beyond.

This was the story.   And as Arthur concluded
the narration he said to his mother, in his most
earnest manner:

"Do you know, mamma, that's just the way I
think it will be with us when we die!"

His mother assured him that she thought it
a very beautiful story, and was glad he had
remembered it so well and believed it to be true
for all of us when the great change comes.

After making his closing remark as given
above,— his confession of hope and faith in the
life beyond,— Arthur seemed satisfied, and went
trustingly to sleep.

How touchingly beautiful are such hope and
faith in a child!   There is in this world nothing
else like it.   How it shames the doubts and
questionings of maturer years!   There is in it
something so pure and sweet, so full of utter
trust and unsuspecting faith, that it would seem
as if the Good God must make it come true so

as not to disappoint these trembling little hearts who have accepted this glorious thought as just the thing He has in store for them.

At any rate, this was Arthur's confident, earnest faith. Although he was not quite thirteen years of age when he first heard this story, the suggestion in it took deep root in his mind. He evidently had thought it over many times, carrying out the applications of the analogy to the experiences and hopes of this human life, and had concluded that this was the way it is to be: that we are to live again in forms different from these earthly bodies, and in a far more beautiful land; and that, while we might wish to come back to earth to revisit our friends and to assure them that we were still living, this gratification of the earthly longing would not be possible since the conditions of life would be so different. The loved ones of earth can go onward and upward, but they cannot return to earthly conditions. The friends left behind must therefore be content to live simply in hope and trust in the beautiful life beyond. Such was Arthur's thought.

And truly, have any of us a better or more rational faith than this? Drawn as is the beautiful analogy from the domain of great Nature, it has a striking force illustrative of the probability, if not the certainty, of man's spiritual destiny. The analogy is surely in Nature as a fact; the conclusion is apparently a just inference. Why, then, should we not be bold enough to apply it? Why may we not believe that the Good God, in this wonderful transformation in the life of a dragon-fly, has given us an object-lesson in spiritual transformation also? If God can so translate and transform the physical life of an insect, why shall he not also translate and transform, in some similar manner, the spiritual nature of man?

Reason as we may, we cannot escape the suggestive force of the analogy. Moreover, when we recall how, through the simple narration of this story, the thought in it appealed so effectively to the mind of a young boy, we must needs believe that it carries with it something sanative and even prophetic, to fresh untrammeled natures. May we not at least cherish the physical fact described as a psychic hint, until we can show it to be an illuminating spiritual demonstration? Emerson says: "The best proof of a heaven to come is its dawning within us now." Nature gives no promise that she does not or will not sometime fulfil; she raises no hungers which she is not prepared to satisfy; she implants no instincts without furnishing also some means for their gratification. I find ever that the most crushing answer I am able to make to my doubts and questionings as to the future life is: If there is none, *there ought to be!* Therefore I am impelled to hold the universe to that degree imperfect and morally unjust, if it does not meet the grand promise in man's spiritual nature with a glorious fulfilment. Uniting reason and analogy, instinct and the moral sense, the thought of continuous spiritual growth and conscious personal existence hereafter comes as the sanest conclusion in a sane world.

When we ponder Arthur's spiritual fate; when we strive to vision the experiences at present being allotted to him by the mighty cosmic "Power not ourselves," now that his physical habitation has fallen into decay, we cannot make any other thought seem so certain to us as that he is "not lost, but gone before"; not destroyed, but transformed; not banished forever from our love, but waiting until we, too, shall leave the physical body behind and, taking on the new

form of the spiritual life, shall once more join
our lives and loves beyond.   Our hearts cry out
for this comfort of humane belief; our reason
pleads constantly its justice; and our faith in
the Eternal Goodness holds us loyal to this great
and ennobling Hope of the world.

Perhaps the belief and feeling in our minds
is most fittingly expressed in that touchingly
human little poem by James Whitcomb Riley,—
"He's Just Away":

> "I cannot say and I will not say
> That he is dead — he's just away.
> With a cheery smile and a wave of his hand,
> He has wandered into an unknown land,
> And left us dreaming how very fair
> It needs must be, since he lingers there.
>
> "And you, O you, who the wildest yearn
> For the old-time step and the glad return —
> Think of him faring on, as dear
> In the love of There as the love of Here;
> Think of him still the same, I say —
> He is not dead — he's just away."

XII.

THE MINISTRY OF HIS LIFE.

Living, our loved ones make us what they dream;
Dead, if they see, they know us as we are.
Henceforward we must be, not merely seem;
Bitterer woe than Death it were by far
To fail their hopes whose love can still redeem;
Loss were thrice loss which thus their faith could mar.
—*Arlo Bates.*

Some things are so preciously true that we long to confess them at once. Moreover, when these things concern another to whom, unconciously to him, we have been indebted for years, we feel the injustice of a merely conventional silence. Why should not men and women reveal to each other, more than they do, the spiritual influences which have been most helpful in their lives? Not to acknowledge the things we owe to others' lives is to lessen human life itself by so much of its goodness.

(90)

The confession I joyously long to make here
is the pervasive and persuasive influence of this
young boy's life upon my own. It is but a simple
statement of fact to say that his ministry for
me began with his babyhood, continued in deep-
ening touches and widening circles as the years
of his boyhood went by, and that now, when
he is no longer present in the flesh, he is yet
moulding me in my spiritual life and blessing
me more richly than I am able to describe.

Emerson has assured us that "What we do
not call education is more precious than that
which we do call so." Our spiritual enlighten-
ment may come from very humble and hidden
sources, and we are the inheritors of and are
moulded by all the spiritual influences touching
our lives. Painful as it is in one sense to confess it, yet I hesitate not to admit that this
young boy's life has been the most helpful
stimulus to my own personal life, the most persuasive teacher of all my years. How has this
great influence been exerted? It is difficult
to explain. I can only state the fact, to me
undeniable, that by the power of intimate companionship, by the simple influence of the goodness regnant in his boy-life, and by the mild

persistence of his gentle spirit, I was won to love the good for its own sake as never before.

It is a difficult and even hopeless task to seek to trace the odor of a flower to its secret dwelling-place in the corolla-shrine of its most delicate life. We are satisfied to look at its sculptured beauty, to enjoy its delicious fragrance, and we shrink from prying into what is so intangible in essence and so exhilarating in its effects. Something of this feeling accompanies the efforts we make to trace subtle personal influences to their origin in the recesses of spiritual character. We feel the sunshine of a personal presence, and we know there must be a source whence the sunshine proceeds. But we stop not to speculate, we linger simply to bask in its genial, life-giving warmth. We feel the touch of contact of a beautiful human spirit in some precious reveal-ment of intimate experience, and the current of a diviner life passes into ours. In this way all of us are the spiritual pensioners of each other's lives. We give and take freely and unconsciously the best gifts, and never know the fullness of the blessings we have given or received.

Children are more natural and transparent than adults, and so their characters are read more surely. This is what we first feel when brought into contact with them. And hence the spirit of a boy's life is quickly manifest and easily felt. The clearness and singleness of the spirit of Arthur's life were self-revealing; one had to be in his presence for a few minutes only to get an unmistakable impression of the kind of a boy he was in truth. Honesty and gentleness, elemental in his nature, were always speaking from his face, his voice, and in his whole manner; and these were irresistible in their winsomeness, in their subtle but pervasive power to affect and attract others. His affection and loyalty were impartial. No selfish consideration or advantage whatever could induce him to take sides with either father or mother as against the other. When the spirit of inharmony obtruded itself for the moment into the usual peacefulness of the home-nest, he suffered keenly while it lasted, and was very careful to add nothing to it by word or action; instead, himself kept the bond of peace unbroken. He was for peace ever, with all the strength and impulse of his calm, self-poised character. He had tasted the blessedness of the beatitude of peace long before he had read it. Thus the silent ministry of his personal influence in our home went on unceasingly.

Perhaps the influence of his life was most helpful to me in those respects in which his character was of finer tissue, of a higher emotional standard than my own. Where his spirit was sanest, and his disposition the more sympathetic, the moulding power of his personal presence was most compelling and permanent. The imperfections and weaknesses of my own character never showed so plainly as when brought into comparison with his almost constant wholesomeness of conduct. Had I a defect exposed for which I suffered? The criticism of his silent possession of the opposite virtue became the most eloquent condemnation of my personal fault. Did I give way to quick feelings and anger? His calm demeanor was always present to remind me of how far I had stepped aside. Did I say and do things unworthy of a wise and true father? The silent look of pitiful pain which swept over his face was convincing testimony that I had done wrong. Only those parents who have suffered a similar experience can know how far-reaching, unforgettable and transforming in their influences and effects upon themselves are such character-ideals when incarnated in the life and conduct of a dearly-beloved child.

By the power of his own unconscious example, and by the demonstration of personal contrast, he was always teaching us as a household the superiority of the better way. We were made to see how beautiful and attractive it was, illustrated in daily life by a boy who so spontaneously lived in the atmosphere of the spiritual life, full of love, sympathy and kindness.

But pervasive and deep-searching as was the influence of his character, gentle and constraining as was the ministry of his spirit while yet with us and moving actively about in the domestic life of which he was so genial a part, yet, now that his personal presence is absent from our lives, his power for good grows still more persuasive and beautiful, and his influence becomes more spiritual and winning than ever. Hopelessly true is it that the well-known boyish form is no longer here; the softly-modulated words we no longer hear; the caressing touch we do not feel, and we long in vain for another look into those luminous, soul-full eyes: but a Presence as of the *real Arthur* seems ever more to be about us. The same spirit, only more self-revealing and ethereal, freer and more joyful, seems to be still carrying on the delicate, silent

work in our midst which he began when a child.
The Arthur whom we but dimly saw before, we
now see with the clearness of spiritual insight.
We thought we knew him while he was with us,
but we now know that we did not see clearly;
our vision was blurred by the physical mediums
of expression; while now, looking through the
eyes of memory washed clear by the tears of a
sweet and hallowed sorrow, we see him more
truly as he was and is. Whenever we invite his
pure spirit to come to us, we can now enter his
real presence at will, unfettered and undisguised
by the fleshly organs of speech and sense. Often
as I walk forth in the fields and woods, or stand
looking over the familiar landscapes, dwelling in
the sweet memories of departed days, he seems
to come and stand beside me with his gentle
hand in mine, or with his arm drawn shyly
through my arm as in the days of closest earthly
companionship, while I impulsively make the
old habitual response. At such moments, giving
myself up to the pure thought and the tender
emotion evoked by the impression of his presence, I stand on hallowed ground, and he comes
nearer to me in spirit and in truth than in
any personal contacts or intimacies to be recalled

in our lives. I seem then in the mood most favorable for the reception of spiritual influences and impressions, and I feel the sympathetic necessity of Tennyson's verse:

> " How pure at heart and sound in head,
>   With what divine affections bold,
> Should be the man whose thought would hold
> An hour's communion with the dead."

At such times Arthur and I are brought very closely together, into a oneness of spirit and understanding such as did not seem possible in the old days of physical separateness and individual personalities. From him there obtrudes now no hindrance of sense to color the soul-impression made, and for the moment I myself seem largely freed from the material bonds of the flesh and of time. The interblending of spiritual thoughts and feelings seems complete, and in this experience I feel that I have been ministered unto by a pure communion with the real Arthur,— with him whom I knew here only in part, though loving him purely and unreservedly. Thus his spirit continues to help and bless me in my highest needs more than I am able to confess, and I write these words here, not because of a conventional license of speech permissible in time of grief, but because they best describe a chapter in the actual emotional experiences of my later years.

We constantly find in life new illustrations of the truth that what we seem to lose is often more than made good to us in what we gain out of the loss.   This is a great spiritual fact, though seemingly paradoxical in its statement; and in the personal experience of sorrow no demonstration of the law of spiritual compensation is more immanent and eloquent.   We who knew him say sometimes, by reason of the habitual iteration of speech, that we have *lost* Arthur, having in mind the sense of our loss of his personal presence, of the inconsolable and ever-present grief at his absence.   And we know that we *have* lost *something* out of our earthly lives and experiences which can never more come back to them.   It is like the memory of a gracious day which, once gone, is gone forever.   The song, half-sung, has been silenced; the fair vision which promised so much has faded away, never in full to be realized. And so the painful, unchangeable fact remains: in physical form and bodily presence we no longer see him; —

" He has disappeared from the Day's eye."

From the haunts that knew him best, there is an unbroken absence of one of the sweetest spirits that ever found itself at home in human organism. We miss the winsome Arthur-boy whom we thought we knew so well; we can no longer look into his glowing eyes, or hold his gentle hand caressingly in ours as in the days departed. We find ourselves longing mournfully and without ceasing

> " For the touch of a vanished hand,
> And the sound of a voice that is still."

But — if there is a "gain to match" and more than match such a loss as this of ours, we are forbidden to call this experience a loss!

And this is what has really occurred. Something incommunicably precious and holy has come forth from it all, which closes our lips from all complaint and makes our sorrow dumb with a secret and subtle consciousness that not to have known *this* experience would have been the greater loss. In place of the physical absence has come a spiritual presence,— the same presence with which we were so familiar in its earthly

tabernacle, but now bodiless, unseen by these
eyes, freed from the organs of the senses, and
become, instead, the pure and inspiring memory
of the royal goodness of a sweet youthful life.
His spirit was with us before, but, through our
blindness, wholly tethered to the earth-plane,
hedged in by his and our own physical limita-
tions, however peering out at us in moments of
deep emotion and speaking to us in the terms of
human affection and endearment. His was a
most gracious spirit modestly appealing to us for
just recognition, even for full appreciation. But
our eyes seemed beholden in those days by the
familiar contacts of time and space and earthly
relationship, and we could not see clearly the
radiant beauty of soul-life enshrined in that boyish figure. His spirit of spontaneous goodness
had diffused itself so gently, so self-forgettingly
for us all, during his youthful life, that its absence
alone brought to us the full realization of its
worth and blessedness.

Now in "diffusion ever more intense" it continues to permeate our whole lives. He is with
us wherever we go and however we abide in
these changing earthly tents which we call
"home." In very delicate personal ways his

life still ministers unto us in unmistakable and deeply spiritual helpfulnesses. He is in all our thoughts to sweeten, elevate and enlarge them. He has become the ideal, sometimes conscious, sometimes unconscious, that draws us ever upward and onward towards the better life possible to us.

The influence of his spirit and of his attitude toward life has touched deeply the springs of ethical conduct and spiritual motive in my own personal life. This fact will scarcely admit of description, being almost too elusive for expression; and yet I am constantly made conscious of it, sometimes painfully, sometimes joyously. I find myself often asking: "What would Arthur have done? How would he have met this obstacle?" And then, without effort, the spirit and example of his habitual conduct rises before me as the standard, and I try to rise to the level of that high attitude. He thus, again and again, becomes incarnated spiritually in my life, and "though dead he yet speaketh," his spirit to mine, his heart full of love to my heart full of need.

The thought of him has become the tenderest reality of my life, filling me with a nameless

longing and hunger for that Ideal Goodness
of which his own life was so inspiringly and
attractively suggestive. I feel that there was
something sweet and pure in him which flowered
forth from the Divine Sweetness and Purity.
This blessed thought calls forth my best impulses
of emulation, and tends to awaken my dormant
possibilities of nobility. It thrills me at times
with an ecstatic emotion which ploughs deep
through the hardened strata of my past habits
and tendencies and leaves me softened and
mellowed and open to all tender and divine
influences.

His was a boy's life "filled with grace and
truth"; and he lived with me in all the mutually
sacred relationships and tender ties of father
and child with reciprocal understanding and
love.

His is now an angel's life, chastening and
exalting my own life with a sorrow indescribably
sweet, holy and helpful.

XIII.

"HOPE, HOPE, HOPE."

What can we do, o'er whom the unbeholden
  Hangs in a night with which we cannot cope?
What but look sunward, and with faces golden
  Speak to each other softly of a hope?
                —*F. W. H. Myers.*

IT was always a struggle with him. Nature's healing influences were continuously more than neutralized by the inroads upon him of malignant diseases. The list of these which he experienced seems almost too long for belief, and when recalled one ceases to wonder that during his few years his life swung like a pendulum between hope and despair. He thus knew what suffering, trouble and disappointment mean, as few grown persons know. But, through all these grievous experiences of his childhood and youth, Arthur was patient, uncomplaining and cheerful.

What this persistent attitude meant to him, and what it cost him, we can estimate when it is recalled that all such experiences are directly opposed to those of healthy childhood, and disastrous to many plans and dreams which naturally bud into promise of fulfilment with the coming of the years of boyhood. "What shall I do now?" "What can I do next?" These were the constantly reiterated questions of his many days of confinement indoors when not too ill to play. He often said that if he could only get through the list of diseases that belong to childhood, then he would have a chance to live and enjoy life; but when the diseases of grown people began to afflict him, he felt that this addition was more than he could endure. Through all, however, of the many postponements of pleasure, and the varied disappointments connected with the loss of many things dear to every healthy boy's heart, he kept up his courage, hoping for the best, looking for final recovery, and trusting that his road, which had been an almost unvarying course of unpleasant and painful experiences, would yet take a turn and pass into the sunshine and cheer of good health and happiness.

There were times, it is true, when even his
strong, persistent hope seemed to fail him, and
at such times he would exclaim: "It doesn't
seem worth while to hold on any longer," or, "I
don't think I can hold on any longer": but this
partial eclipse of his patience and fortitude
would only be temporary. A little sympathy, a
few words of cheerful assurance, and the pre-
dominant sunshine of his hope would again
shine forth to gladden us all. Where else can
such patience and faith be found as in the lives
of children? The virtues represented in the
calendar of the saints would, I believe, pale
beside the simple recital of the heroic denials
and touching saintliness of conduct evinced by
childhood.

Thus Arthur lived in and by Hope. He had
learned the need and value of it; he had learned
to look for its beautiful coming, to prize its
cheerful face, remembering how frequently it
had saved him from dark days and gloomy
prospects by its timely arrival and uplifting
presence. This Hope was it which fed his
hungry heart when his patience became weary
and the thing he had so longed for seemed to
slip farther and farther away till it disappeared

from sight. What a gospel of good news and cheer did this young boy thus preach to those about him, as, rising above each new disappointment, he let the glad Hope that was in his heart shine forth from his face and sing clear in the tones of his voice!

This example of Arthur's is left us now to cheer our remaining years with Hope. This is to be the continuance, in part, of the gracious ministry of his life — the eternally cheering assurance rising in our hearts that there is something in human life so pure and good that, if we can but attain to it, or even journey towards it, the striving for it will be supremely worth our while; and that through all life's minor, earthly strains of discouragement there is to be heard as the key-note of it all this brave major tone of heavenly Hope.

Yet this faith that now holds in its loving embrace our greatest sorrow, and leaves it unembittered, has been bought with a great price of spiritual wrestling and agony. With the gathering of the Death-Shadow and the consciousness of what it bore away out of my life, there came to me, until the shadow passed, mental conflicts and soul-struggles which threatened to lead me into the land of Despair and there leave me alone in my misery. My former edifice of faith was rent and rocked to its very foundation-stones. Doubts surged in and mocked at my firm beliefs, and it seemed at times as if my innermost conviction of the moral saneness of the universe would be torn up by the roots. Is there a good God? Is there eternal justice? How can He think it best, or right, thus rudely to break tenderest human ties by taking our loved ones away from us? These embittered interrogatories of freshly-made sorrow pressed upon me, and my despoiled soul was thrown back upon itself for answer. The fantasies of materialism joined in the attack upon my faith in the spiritual verities of the universe, and the conclusions of reason, whether on this side or that, were quickly overborne by opposing revulsions of feeling, until all things seemed uncertain, all thought useless, and the so-called realities of life only fictions of the imagination. This storm of doubt and questioning swept over my soul's anchorage in the historical faith of the past and in the intuitive faith of the present, and left me desolate. Could the serene faith of Jesus, eighteen hundred years ago, satisfy the longing anguish of my bereaved heart here and now? Where was Arthur? What was his fate? Had he a home, and had he found a father and mother in the spirit-life? Did he live in a Celestial Country whose glory and happiness so exceeded those of the land he had left that, perhaps like some of the dragon-flies, he was too happy to wish to return? — or was he powerless to do as he wished? *How was it in truth?* Looking up into the clear face of the sky at night, into those depths of stars glittering in the visible heavens, God's handiwork, my heart's hunger compelled me to ask again and again: "Oh, where art thou to-night, dearest Arthur-boy — where, where?" The universe seemed so very large, such infinite spaces were on every hand, that in the midst of all its wide freedom and illimitable beauty he might become entranced, lost in wonder and happiness at the newness and glory of it all, and forget — possibly forget ——!

But I could not feel that he would forget us. And yet this ignorance — this ignorance!

Over and over again these thoughts and doubts and questionings thronged through my mind, until they seemed to have worn grooves in the fibres of my brain so that everything about which I tried to think turned at length into these deep-cut channels of the mental experience through which I was passing.

The star which rose at last over this waste of troubled spiritual waters was that star of Hope which had shone over the whole of Arthur's life. As for him it had gleamed amid all his deprivation and suffering, so now it came at length to spread its mild and cheering light over my own heart's desolation. Well-founded reason may come to reassure; the moral sense may help to preserve self-poise; faith may bring courage: but it is Hope which gives peace and comfort and will not let the heart break.

Moreover, *his* hope helps our hope. If he could be brave and cheerful, so ought we to be. And thus, when we would complain, silence falls upon us and grief is swallowed up in the joy of our Great Hope.

Among the many helpful and comforting letters we received after Arthur had gone, were

these beautiful and compassionate words from a
brother-minister : —

"And so the great trial has come to you both
again.   That you will both meet it bravely I do
not for a moment doubt; but the finest courage
will not take away the heart-ache of these days,
and I wish I might look into your faces and
thus say to you silently what I have not words
to express.

> 'What is excellent,
>   As God lives, is permanent'

keeps running in my head, and so I put it
down; and then the beautiful words sing on:

> 'Hearts are dust, hearts' loves remain,
>   Heart's love will meet thee again.'

But all this and much more you have already
said to yourselves, and still the mystery remains.
All we can really do is to light it up with Hope,
and at times we must wait even for her coming.
But her beautiful face is sure to shine for you
both again, by and by, and you will again be
'at peace about God and about death.'"

And so it was, and is. Hope's beautiful face shines again, and we know now why it is true that

"'Tis better to have loved and lost
Than never to have loved at all."

This same key-note of hope, as shown in Arthur's life, was pathetically referred to at the final service at the church where he had spent so many happy hours, when appreciative and affectionate words were spoken by one who had known of the disappointments of Arthur's life, and how he had exhibited through it all such undying faith and courage. These words of final farewell had the touching impressiveness of the simple truth:

"And now that Arthur's earthly life is ended, what better word of benediction can I leave with you, sorrowing friends, than that which was *the inspiration of his life,*— Hope, Hope, Hope."

I have found much comfort and inspiration in often standing beside that spot of hallowed ground where we laid to rest his earthly dust. This mound has served to us as the visible link binding his earth-life to our thought of that new experience into which he has entered. The hours there have taught me many things; in them I have found great help.

One day as I thus stood, with the sense of loss and desolation sweeping over me and the sadness and loneliness of the years to come rising into a dumb kind of consciousness, these words came to me as if whispered by *him* for my soul's need:

"Through all the coming years, papa, just be glad."

It was as if his Presence stood beside me and sang the words over and over again. They have ever since recurred to me at need, and have become the benediction of my life.

The little poem of Riley's where the words occur teaches such a blessed lesson of gladness for the life that now is ours, that it is given here entire:

> "O heart of mine, we shouldn't
>   Worry so !
>   What we've missed of calm we couldn't
>   Have, you know !
>   What we've met of stormy pain
>   And of sorrow's driving rain,

We can better meet again
    If it blow.

‘ We have erred in that dark hour,
    We have known,
When the tears fell with the shower
    All alone.
Were not shine and shower blent
As the gracious Master meant?
Let us temper our content
    With his own.

" For we know, not every morrow
    Can be sad.
So, forgetting all the sorrow
    We have had,
Let us fold away our fears,
And put by our foolish tears,
And through all the coming years
    Just be glad."

XIV.

"O FAIR, CHASTE SAINT."

Yet, though thou wear'st the glory of the sky,
  Wilt thou not keep the same beloved name,
The same fair thoughtful brow and gentle eye,
  Lovelier in heaven's sweet climate, yet the same?
                                        —*Bryant.*

ONE day in the latter part of May, in an old
  Vermont apple-orchard, years ago, a strange,
new bird alighted, and in an alert, frightened
way looked around. Its plumage was pure white;
its neck was long, its wings large, and it had a
tapering head with piercingly bright eyes. It
sat still long enough for a young boy to recognize
with wonder these unusual features of its appear-
ance, and then it flew away into the unknown
South. Its glistening white form, reflecting the
bright sunshine, made the boy feel sure that this
bird was a visitant from another clime, perhaps
from another world. Evidently the venturesome
bird had strayed far from its native haunts, and

was now returning, tired and homesick. But the wondrous, indelible, mystical impression made by it upon that farmer-boy's youthful imagination still remains. He wondered what species of bird it was, its reason for wandering into this inland country, and what a surprising history it might tell of its travels and experiences. It seemed to him to resemble a sea-bird of some kind; it was perhaps most like pictures of sea-gulls he had seen. And then he thought of the sea, of what it must be like, and of the strange life possibly lived there by this bird. To him it was both a visitor and a messenger from that new and unseen world to which his thoughts had been carried — that other world of shore and sea which to his imagination seemed entrancingly beautiful.

As it was with this bird, may it sometimes be with souls? Do they at times get beyond their natural habitat, and into uncongenial surroundings? Tender hearts here among us, sympathetic lives, loving whatever is good and pure and noble — do they not seem sometimes to have wandered into this life from a country elsewhere,— visitors from that Other World, and as yet not acclimated to this? How we look upon them — different in many ways, it would seem, from ourselves, though closely related to us; and we wonder if we are to become like them. How nobly these lives affect us, — so pure in thought, so good and kind in action, so gentle in voice and manner! We look on them to admire, and cannot wholly do away with the thought that they may be the lost inhabitants of another sphere.

When one of these suddenly leaves us some day, unexpectedly, we are startled and pained that the fair vision, *the white soul*, has gone from us. At the same time, we seem to have a strangely instinctive feeling that the spiritually beautiful life belonged to another clime than ours, and so has only gone home, leaving us with the memory of its gracious presence.

Fair, white-souled messengers, dwelling with us for a few short years of earthly life! may we not again greet you, in some home-like spot somewhere on the shores of the Greater Ocean?

How tenderly we recall the impressions made upon us in those last days when Arthur was unconsciously loosening his hold of the earth-life! His mother thus described the pathos of it all when Arthur had passed on:

"But he wanted to go to school, and kept it up until the spring vacation, when he gave up and stayed at home with mother for three short months. I wish you might have seen him; he grew so beautiful and sweet, his eyes so luminous and bright. As I look back it seems like caring for an angel whose delicate body was too frail for this coarse environment. How happy he must be in a more congenial clime! I used to say to him: 'Arthur, if you leave me, I must go too.' But here I am, trying to wait until my work is done, praying for strength."

Arthur's young life reminds us of the glory and promise of a bright spring morning; the remembrance of it has become a beautiful fragrance wafted over the hills and vales of the past by the soft breezes of memory. He lived only sixteen years, but in that time he had learned the secret of the Beautiful Life, and lived it each day. His spirit surely adorned with a rare grace the life into which it was sent.

That he has wandered into the deep glens of Paradise is our sorrow, but it is a golden sorrow. I am more grateful for this boy's life — that it was spared to me even so long as it was — than I can find utterance for. I am so much the better man because he lived. His spirit has wooed and won me, and I, too, must seek the Highest.

> "O fair, chaste saint, so calm, so true;
>   Art thou my sometime fate?
> How strong my will, how brave my heart,
>   To work and wait."

Arthur C. Stevens,
June 25, 1881 — June 22, 1897.

www.ingramcontent.com/pod-product-compliance
Lightning Source LLC
Chambersburg PA
CBHW020759020726
47495CB00008B/2509